It was wrong to ~~stare~~*. But I couldn't help myself. I didn't want to tear my eyes away. Not when she looked so tempting. So ravishing.*
ANGELINO VALENTINO

DIRTY SHAME

A Corrupted Angels Prequel to Defy Me

C. DAVIS

Copyright ©

2020 C. Davis-
All rights reserved

No part of this publication may be reproduced, distributed, or transmitted in an form or by any means, including photocopying, recording, or other electronic or mechanical methods, without the prior written permission of the publisher, except in the case of brief quotations embodied in critical reviews and certain other non-commercial uses permitted by the copyright law.

This is a work of fiction. All names, characters, places and specific instances are products of the author's imagination and used fictitiously. No actual reference to any real person, living or dead, is intended or inferred.

Contents

Dirty Shame

Prologue
Chapter 1
Chapter 2
Chapter 3
Chapter 4
Chapter 5
Chapter 6
Chapter 7
Chapter 8
Chapter 9
Chapter 10
Chapter 11
Chapter 12
Chapter 13
Chapter 14
Chapter 15
Copyright

She's the forbidden fruit. I'm just a bad apple. Rotten to the core. I know it's wrong, but I can't stop my eyes from lingering longer than I'm supposed to.

I'm a bad boy for looking.

She's my best friend's sister. Not to be corrupted. Off limits to everyone. Myself included.

The bad part?

She knows how tempting she is.

Flaunts her body. Teases me with her deep blue eyes and her filthy mouth. She wants me. Wants me to defile her. I'm screwed. Royally screwed.

Why?

Because I really want to. No matter what, I can't crack. Can't give in and lose my self-control.

But how can I when she tests me?

It's only a matter of time until I snap. Bend the Princess over my knee and spank her. Punish her real good. Make her my good girl.

Prologue

Angelo

"Don't you want me, Angelo?" Vivianna asked.

God yes, more than anything.

But she's Matteo's little sister.

Do. Not. Touch. Her.

"Put your clothes back on. Or else..."

"I know you want me. Would it help if..."

"Dammit, Vivianna. Put your goddamn clothes back on or I'll have to punish you."

Her eyes lit up as she turned around and bent over my desk. She glanced over her shoulder and whispered. "Punish me, Daddy."

Lord, please send help.

Tie my hands behind my back, so I don't touch her.

I did the one thing I could think of. I walked away from temptation. Out of my own damn office and into my bedroom. I glanced down at my hard cock and whispered. "Not today, Satan. Not today."

Satan-0

Me-1

Chapter 1

Angelo

I glanced at Matteo and nodded as he took a seat in front of me. I knew him well enough to know this wasn't a social call. He needed something from me. A favor.

"What can I do for you?" I asked.

Matteo let out a long sigh. "My sister, she... I hate to ask you of this. Would it be okay if she stays here? Just until I figure something out."

"Sister?"

This was the first hearing about close family. Of course, there's his cousin Roman. I've never once heard him talk of a sister.

"I had to bail her out of jail last night. Apparently, she tried to bust the tigers out of the zoo."

Tigers, huh?

"We're family, yes?"

"Yes, boss." Matteo replied.

"I'll have Carmella prepare a room for her."

"Are you sure? Vivianna can be quite difficult at times."

I waved him off.

"Any family of yours is family of mine. How old is she?"

"Seventeen."

Barely legal.

Well, fuck me.

"Should I lock the liquor cabinet?"

"That would be advisable, boss."

"I'll arrange a car to pick her up. All I need is an address."

Matteo chuckled softly. "About that, I should be the one to pick her up. She's not going to be very happy when she finds out my plan."

I raised a brown in question.

"She's a brat, but she's still my sister. I might have to use force to get her here."

"You're going to drug her?" I questioned.

"If it comes to that, but I hope it doesn't." Matteo answered.

"Go. When you get back, bring her to me. I have some rules for her."

Matteo gave me a single nod and stepped out. I took off my jacket and loosened my tie. My finger pressed the intercom button. "Carmella, prepare a room. I'm expecting a guest."

"Yes, Sir." She answered.

Seventeen.

I chanted over and over in my head.

She's seventeen.

Off limits.

Best friend/ second-in-command's kid sister.

Maybe she'll be ugly. I laughed at myself. No way in hell she'd be hideous. Not with her being a Fiorentino. Just look at Matteo. Devilishly handsome. I'm not gay, but he is. So is Roman. Maybe she'll be disgusting.

I poured a glass of whiskey and took a drink to calm my nerves.

Satan taunted me.

You know she won't be ugly.

I took another drink.

Fuck!

Best friend's sister.

Off limits.

Do. Not. Touch.

I cleared my throat when I heard a knock at the door.

"Enter."

Vito opened the door for Matteo. In his arms, he carried the most beautiful woman I'd ever laid eyes on. I was fucked. So. Damn. Screwed. Matteo laid her on the sofa and let out a frustrated breath. "She didn't go lightly, so I had to sedate her."

"Go put her in the guest room next to yours." I commanded him. I don't think I need to say this, but I'm going to anyway. Don't fuck my sister. Make sure everyone else knows that too."

"Never. She's not my type. Too blonde for me."

That was a damn lie. Vivianna was exactly my type. That's why I needed to keep my distance. If I got within reach, I would touch her. Fuck her. Claim every inch of her body.

It's been a few days since Vivianna has started staying here. So far, I'd successfully avoided her like the damn plague. I'd yet to go over the rules. I don't know how many times I've used Carmella only to pretend it was Vivianna. Hell, I wished it was her.

That's your best friend's sister, perv.

Don't think of her like that.

I sighed when I heard a soft knock at my bedroom door. I swallowed hard when I opened the door. There she was looking all…

Fuck me.

"Miss Vivianna, how can I help you?"

"Mr. Valentino, I wanted to come personally thank you for letting me stay here."

"It's no problem." I muttered.

Vivianna pushed her way into my room and shut the door. She placed her hands on my chest and ran down my body, stopping at my belt. "Let me thank you properly."

Matteo was right. This girl is a troublemaker. T-R-O-U-B-L-E. A bad girl. Very bad girl. All I want to do is bend the Princess over my knee and spank her for being a damn tease.

Don't give in, Angelo.

Fight the urge.

I grabbed each of her wrists and pinned them to her sides. "Stop, a thank you is fine. While you're here, I want to go over my rules."

Vivianna rolled her eyes and scoffed.

"Rule number one, don't roll your eyes at me. If you were anyone else, you'd be lying in a pool of your own blood."

"Rules?" Another eye roll. "I thought you were cool. Big. Bad. Man."

"I am cool, but you're underage and lack discipline and respect. Rule number two, no alcohol and drugs."

"And what happens if I break one of those rules?" Vivianna teased.

"You really don't want to find out, Princess."

"But if I did, would you punish me?"

I closed my eyes and cursed under my breath. "Rule number three, do as I say."

"Let's say I'm drunk, would you bend me over and spank me? Punish me for being a naughty little girl?"

Christ!

This is absolute torture.

If only she knew.

"Obey the rules, and we won't have a problem. Be a good little girl and do as I say. Be a bad girl and I'll be forced to tell Matteo. Dinner is served at six o'clock sharp. Don't be late."

"Yes, Daddy."

"Don't say shit like that." I hissed.

Vivianna pressed up against me and whispered. "Don't you like it when I call you that, Daddy?"

"No!" I growled. "I don't."

That's a lie. I loved hearing her call me that.

"But your dick seems to like it. It's so hard, Daddy."

"Go to your room. Now!" I demanded. "I don't want to see you until dinner."

She pouted. "Fine."

Thankfully, she obeyed. But now, I had a problem. My dick was raging mad at me. Hard as steel.

I stormed towards my office and called for Carmella. She entered and locked the door. She knew what I needed.

"Knees, sweetheart. I need your mouth."

Carmella sunk to her knees as I freed my cock. She eagerly took me in her mouth. Sucked me greedily.

"Fuck, sweetheart. That's a good girl." I groaned.

I wrapped my hand around her blonde hair, forcing more into her mouth. Tilting my head back, I closed my eyes and moaned. I imagine it's Vivianna's sweet mouth sucking me off. Taking every inch. Gagging on my dick. Whimpering for Daddy.

My hips jerked as I spilled into Carmella's mouth. When I opened my eyes, Carmella cleaned the rest of my cum with her tongue.

I helped her up and whispered. "Thank you. Meet me in my room after dinner."

"It's her, isn't it?" Carmella asked.

"I don't know what you're talking about."

"If you want, you can pretend I'm her. I can…"

"Enough. You can go now. Remember, my room after dinner."

"Of course, Mr. Valentino."

"And not a word to anyone."

"Yes, Sir."

Another knock sounded on the door.

Vivianna entered and let her dress fall off her body.

I swallowed hard and averted my gaze.

"Don't you want me, Angelo?" Vivianna asked.

God yes, more than anything.

But she's Matteo's little sister.

Do. Not. Touch. Her.

"Put your clothes back on. Or else…"

"I know you want me. Would it help if…"

"Dammit, Vivianna. Put your goddamn clothes back on or I'll have to punish you."

Her eyes lit up as she turned around and bent over my desk. She glanced over her shoulder and whispered. "Punish me, Daddy."

Lord, please send help.

Tie my hands behind my back, so I don't touch her.

I did the one thing I could think of. I walked away from temptation. Out of my own damn office and into my bedroom. I glanced down at my hard cock and whispered. "Not today, Satan. Not today."

Satan-0

Me-1

Chapter 2

Vivianna

I was pissed. No. Not pissed. That didn't even cover it. Lying bastard tricked me. He bailed me out of jail and made me think he was taking me to Roman's place. Matteo Goddamn Fiorentino pulled a fast one on me. He stuck me in the neck with a needle and knocked me out. The next time I woke up, I was in a massive house. Apparently, my brother thinks it's best if I lived under the same roof as him.

Fuck Matteo.

And fuck his sexy boss.

No.

Not sexy.

An asshole.

Matteo's boss wants me to live by rules. His rules. You know what I say about rules? Rules were made to be broken.

I checked my appearance in the mirror. Perfect. Surely, I can talk one of Angelo's men and seduce some booze or weed out of them. I stepped out of the room to be met with one of his goons. Cue the eye roll. He kept his expression Stoic and avoided looking at me.

"Dinner will be served in ten minutes." He muttered.

"What's your name, big boy?" I purred, looking him up and down.

"Not important." He grumbled.

"You know, we still have ten minutes. I could…"

"Vivianna!" Matteo hissed. "That's quite enough."

I rolled my eyes.

Too bad Angelo wasn't here to witness this.

One rule broken.

You hear me, Angelo?

Rule broken.

Eat that, asshole.

Matteo grabbed me by the elbow, dragging me down the hall.

"Ouch, that hurts!" I growled. "Let. Me. Go."

Matteo stopped and pushed me firmly against the wall. I glared. He challenged my glare and narrowed his eyes. He leaned into my neck and whispered harshly in my ear. "You best be on good behavior. Angelo Valentino isn't a man to be fucked with. You will now, say please and thank you, and keep your attitude to a minimum. Do I make myself clear, Princess?"

"Fuck you."

"Watch it, Vivianna. If you can't behave, you can march right back to your room for the rest of the night. It's your choice."

"Fine. I'll be a good little girl and be the perfect Princess, brother."

"Good choice." Matteo muttered under his breath.

I yanked my arm out of his hold and stormed into the dining room. When I took my seat, I growled in frustration. A hand clamped down on my shoulder and a familiar voice whispered in my ear. "Fancy meeting you here, cuz."

"Roman!" I squealed. "Finally, someone I can tolerate."

"I left a surprise in your room. Swiped it from Matteo when he wasn't looking. The Finest whiskey." Roman whispered so no one could hear.

Angelo took his seat. Right across from me. I rolled my eyes.

"That's one, Princess." Angelo mouthed, lifting his index finger.

I discreetly flipped him off. He cocked his head to the side as he lifted two fingers.

Roman leaned over and warned me to stop. There was no way Angelo would lay a finger on me. Surely not. Right?

The way his eyes darkened tells me otherwise. So, maybe that wasn't too smart on my behalf.

I raised up from my chair, but my brother me back down. "Don't be rude, sister. Stay. Eat. Have dinner with everyone."

"I-I'm not feeling too good. Maybe it was the drugs, brother."

Roman glanced at me and covered for me. "She does look a little flushed."

"If she's not feeling well, she can be excused." Angelo stated.

I stood up and faked a stumble. Roman was quick to catch me. Just as we walked past Angelo, he threw me a wink.

"Fuck him." I muttered under my breath.

"What the hell was that?!" Roman questioned when we reached my temporary room.

"Nothing." I answered.

Roman raised his brow.

"Angelo may have given me some rules."

"And you probably just broke them all."

I nodded as I looked for the bottle Roman hid for me.

"Under the pillow, Viv."

I reached under the pillow and twisted the cap off. Taking a generous drink, I sighed in satisfaction.

"Wait a minute, Angelo gave you rules?"

"Yes. Apparently, I can't do anything but breathe."

"You could come stay with me. I've got room."

"No can do. Matteo wants to keep me close to him."

"Damn, cuz. I guess you're officially on lock down."

"I'll be just…"

"Roman, I think Matteo needs to speak to you." Angelo told him.

Liar.

"Of course, I'll catch you later, Viv."

I closed my eyes and sucked in a breath. I'd rolled my eyes at Angelo earlier. Twice. Broken his precious rule. Now, I'm breaking the alcohol rule.

"Turn around, Miss Vivianna."

I turned around and hid the bottle behind my back.

"Give me the bottle." He demanded.

"No! You're not the boss of me."

Angelo twisted me around and shoved me down on the bed. He pried the bottle from my hands, slamming it onto the nightstand. "You're acting like a brat. You break my rules. Defy me. Test my patience. Do you know what I'd do if you were one of my men?"

I shook my head ferociously.

"I'd kill them nice and slow until they begged for their death." Angelo hissed. "But for you, I'd just punish you"

"W-what?"

"I. Would. Punish. You. Princess."

"P-punish me?" I stammered.

"Yes, little girl. I'd take my belt off and give you a spanking you'd never forget. You broke three rules. So… I suppose you deserve nine spanks from my leather. Three for each rule you broke."

"Y-you can't do that!" I shrieked.

"I'm the boss, Kitten. I can do anything I want. My house. My rules. My punishments."

"Matteo…"

"Is away for the day. Duty calls, Princess."

I'm fucked.

Roman is gone and so is Matteo.

You can't touch me. Someone will hear."

"Not if I rip your panties off and stuff them in your mouth. Gag you while I whip that pretty little ass until it glows."

I would be lying if I said his threat didn't turn me on. The thought of being at his mercy made me wet.

I gasped when Angelo ripped my panties off and stuffed them into my mouth. I whimpered when he held my hips in place and murmured. "Don't test me, Princess. I'll let you off with a warning this time. Next time, I'll give you fifteen spanks from my belt."

With that being said, he stormed off. Leaving me out of breath. Completely sexually frustrated.

I spit the panties out of my mouth and groaned. He'd taken the liquor with him. Well, it was good while it lasted. I walked to the door and turned the knob. The bastard locked me inside.

"Now, it's officially jail." I whispered to myself.

I laid down on the bed and closed my eyes. Angelo was so determined to punish me.

So, why did he stop?

Angelo doesn't seem like the type of man to back down on his threats. His promise to punish someone. He probably gets off on inflicting pain. I drifted off to sleep with one thing on my mind.

Angelo Valentino.

Dark and dangerous green eyes.

Forbidden.

Off limits to me.

You know what they say about forbidden, right?

It never felt so good.

So. Right.

Chapter 3

Angelo

Christ!

What's my problem?

Oh yeah, now I remember.

The damn tease living under my roof.

I had one rule.

One. Fucking. Rule.

Do not touch her.

Angelo-1

Satan-1

Satan won that round.

Now, I need to beat him in the next one.

Holy shit!

Vivianna Fiorentino isn't as innocent as her brother thinks. No. She's the damn Devil. Satan disguised as a Princess.

"Fuck you, Satan. Fuck. You." I groaned to myself, banging my head on the wall.

Was I really thinking about touching her?

Maybe.

Probably.

Hell. Yes.

I wanted her more and more each day.

I was brought out of my thoughts by a knock my door. I opened it to see Vito nervously rubbing the back of his neck.

"Boss, there's been talk of a traitor amongst us." He muttered.

"Who?!"

"They are saying it's Matteo's sister.," he whispered.

"Find the source and bring them to me." I growled.

"What about the girl?" he asked.

"Leave her to me. If it's true, I'll flush it out of her."

"B-but Matteo…"

"Does not find out. Find out who started it and leave the feisty kitten to me."

Matteo's sister couldn't be a rat. She just couldn't. Whoever said it was a liar. No way was sweet little Vivianna a traitor. I stepped out of my room and stood at her door. I pulled out the key and unlocked it. I could barge in, but I chose not to. Out of respect for Matteo. I knocked. Just in case she was indecent.

"Open up, Vivianna." I said through the door.

No answer.

When I opened the door, I bit back a groan. Vivianna was naked with her fingers thrusting in and out of her little pussy. I tried to look away. Tried was the keyword. I couldn't. My dick was hard. Again. I tried to calm myself. Nothing was helping. Hell, she probably didn't even hear me enter the room.

"Miss Vivianna, put your clothes back on. You and me, we need to have a chat."

"Mmm, Daddy Angelo." Vivianna moaned, throwing her head back.

This is wrong.

Look away, Angelo.

Look the hell away.

I couldn't though. I felt jealous of her fingers. I wanted to be balls deep inside her.

"Dammit girl, put your fucking clothes back on!" I hissed.

"Do you like this, Daddy?" she teased.

"No!"

I did like it.

A little too much.

But she didn't need to know that.

"Hmm, are you gay?"

I closed my eyes tight and pinched the bridge of my nose. She can't be this oblivious, could she? I mean, she has no idea how much she affects me. My body. My control. And my dick? It's hard as hell. My balls are full. Heavy. Ready to cum all over her pretty face.

I opened my eyes and took a deep breath.

"I'm not gay. Clothes. Put. Them. On."

"Oh fuck, Daddy. I'm almost there."

It's a good thing Matteo is gone. That Vito is busy. Because it looks like I'm going to have to put the Princess in her place.

My fingers wrapped around her wrist and jerked on it, causing her to whimper. Bad move on my part. Why? Because I could smell her arousal off her fingers. It was like I was under a spell. You ever seen one of those vampire shows? You know, the one where a newly turned vampire is thirsting for blood for the first time. That's me. Instead of blood, I'm hungry for Vivianna's sweet virgin pussy.

"Finish me, Daddy." She pleads.

"No." I growled. "You and I need to talk. Now!"

The Devil is whispering to me again.

Taste her, Angelo.

Wrap your lips around her fingers and devour her.

"Please, Angelo. Make me cum."

I shook me head.

"No?" Vivianna pouted. "Fine, I'll just do it myself. I've got two hands for a reason."

Before I know it, I've got her pinned down to the bed. A gasp escapes her lips when my body presses against hers. There's only the barrier of my pants separating my dick and her pussy. Her hot, naked heat ready to be taken.

Just one…

Nope.

Not doing it.

Control yourself.

Remember control.

Vivianna's icy blue eyes meet mine as she struggles to break free.

"If I were you, I'd be very still." I warned.

"What?" she whispered.

"If you keep moving, I won't be held responsible for my actions, Princess. Now, if I let you go, will you be a good girl for me?"

"Yes," she murmured.

"Good. And for fuck's sake, put some clothes on."

I released her and turned away. Even though I'd already seen her body, I still turned around.

Fuck me, I almost snapped and had my way with her.

I turned around and sighed in relief when she'd put on a pair of sweats and a shirt.

"What are you doing here?" I questioned.

"What do you mean? Matteo brought me here."

"Who are you working for?" I hissed.

"Nobody."

I took a step forward and cupped her jaw. "I have eyes and ears everywhere, Princess. If I find out you 're lying and are a spy, I'll make sure you never see the light of day."

"I'm not a rat and I don't work at all. To answer the first question, I'm here because Matteo brought me here. I wanted to stay with Roman, but he said no way. I swear to you I'm telling the truth."

I swallowed hard and whispered. "I believe you. Then…"

Was it possible someone was after her? Matteo? Me?

"I'm sorry." Vivianna apologized.

"From now on, you're to be heavily guarded. Vito will be your escort. And when he can't, stay by your brother's side. And when Matteo is away, you will stick with me."

"But…"

"Princess, don't fight me on this."

"Am I in danger?"

"I'm not sure. Just promise me you'll do as I say. If I tell you to run, you fucking run and don't look back. And if I tell you to hide, you hide without hesitation. Understood?"

"Yes, Daddy."

"For God's sake, stop calling me that. If Matteo heard you say that, he'd start asking questions."

"Questions? There's nothing going on. We're… just friends, right?"

"Right. Just friends."

The words "just friends" made me sick. I didn't want to be just a friend. I wanted Vivianna to be my Queen. To me, Vivianna wasn't a little girl. She was all woman. Age was nothing but a number to me. Even if she is only seventeen. However, she'll be eighteen soon.

Vivianna hugged me tight and kissed my cheek. You'll protect me, right?"

"Yes, Princess. I'll do everything in my power to keep you safe."

I pulled away, afraid the Devil might appear on my shoulder.

"Stay here and I'll get you something to drink."

"Wine?"

"Just one glass."

"Such a rebel, Mr. Valentino. It looks like you just broke one of your rules."

With her… I broke all the rules.

"Only with you, Princess. Only with you."

And it was true.

Vivianna was going to be my weakness. Bring the almighty King to his knees.

I would protect her.

But no matter what… I could never cross that line and keep her for myself.

Chapter 4

Vivianna

I couldn't believe it. Angelo was actually bending the rules for me. Letting me have alcohol.

Maybe he's not so bad.

"Drink up, you're going to need it." Angelo told me.

I raised a brow.

"Why?"

"Because I still need to punish you."

I squeezed my thighs together at the thought of his rough hands spanking my bare ass. Bending me over his knee and punishing me for breaking his rules.

"I thought you said you couldn't touch me."

"I only promised Matteo I wouldn't fuck you. That leaves spanking you and making sure you're a good girl while you're in my care."

"Angelo..."

He took the glass from me and set it on the table. His fingers circled my neck and pulled me closer.

"You're not so innocent, are you? You are a bad girl that loves to be punished, yes?"

"Yes," I whispered. "I'm a bad girl for Daddy."

"Fuck, you are very dirty. Tell me, do you crave the dominance or is it the rush when I touch you like this?"

Angelo leaned closer as he ran his finger up my thigh. "Or is it the excitement when you beg Daddy for more? I bet your panties are soaked for him."

"Yes."

"Shit, Vivianna." he cursed. "You're playing with fire. Do you really want Daddy to come out to punish you?"

"You said so yourself. I lack obedience. So, teach me. Please, Daddy."

"Careful what you wish for, Princess. You just might get more what you bargained for."

Angelo pats his thigh. I never look away as I scoot over on his lap. He wraps one arm around my waist and cups my cheek. His touch makes me feel something I'd never felt before. He was right. I craved the dominance. Yearned to be his good girl. I wanted to feel his body against mine as he takes me from behind.

"Ang..."

"Beg me, Princess. I want to hear the words. Tell Daddy how much you crave him."

"Daddy, please." I begged. "Punish me."

"Punish you?"

"I deserve to be spanked."

"Shall I throw you over my knee and yank your pants down? Or... do you want me to throw you on the bed and tie you up so you can't touch yourself?"

"Spank me, Daddy. I've been a naughty princess."

"Yes, you have. And Daddy loves it when you're a bad girl. But right now, I have to refrain myself. And you do too."

"Why?"

"Because your brother could be back any moment now. We don't want him hearing you beg Daddy to spank you harder, do we?"

I shook my head.

"But I do have an idea. After dinner, I want you to meet me in the library. I have a special lesson for you."

"Matteo..."

"Will never know. You know he never goes there. Besides, I have a feeling he'll be busy with something else."

"I have to go deal with some business, but I'll have a guard at the door. And Vivianna? Don't flirt with him to get alcohol. You want something? You ask me first. If you're a good girl, I'll allow another glass of wine. Be bad and I'll deny you. Spank that pretty ass and make sure you can't sit down for weeks."

"I'll be good, Daddy." I whispered.

"I know, Princess. But something tells me you're going to be a bad girl."

"I'll be good." I whispered.

Angelo gathers my hair in his hand and jerks my head back. His eyes darken as he forced my head to the side. "But Daddy really hopes you'll be bad for him. He loves it when his Princess defies him. It makes his dick throb and balls ache when he knows he gets to punish his little girl."

"You do?"

"I'm banking on you to step out of line. I got a brand-new belt with your name on it."

I gasped when he shifted to grind his hardness into my ass. "Oh Daddy, you're so hard."

"Only for you, baby girl. Now I'm wishing I'd sent Matteo away for the week. Dinner is going to be pure torture for me. I won't be able to touch you. Feel this little ass against my dick."

"But you're the boss. You can do anything you want." I argued.

"Using my own words against me, eh? Maybe I should cancel dinner and go straight to dessert. Lock you up and send your brother on a mission to keep him occupied."

He loosened his grip on my waist to reach under my shirt. My vision blurred. Desire spread throughout my body as he inched his way up my belly. I leaned back and closed my eyes when his rough hand cupped my right breast.

"Daddy, please." I whimpered.

Angelo's thumb brushed against my pebbled nipple, making me whimper his name. Not Angelo. Daddy. The name that makes him lose himself.

"I should clamp these and make them nice and hard." Angelo says as he releases my breast. I grind my hips as he takes the puckered bud between his thumb and index finger, giving it a sharp pinch.

"Owww, Daddy." I hissed.

"Ok, I'll stop."

"No! I mean, please don't stop. You just surprised me."

Pinch.

Roll.

Tug.

Twist.

"How about this? You be a good girl at dinner and Daddy will reward you. That means no attitude, no teasing me, and no looking at my men."

"I promise."

Pinch.

Roll.

Tug.

Twist.

"Say it." Angelo growled. "Repeat what I just said."

"I'll be a good girl at dinner for Daddy. That means no attitude, no teasing me, and no looking at his men."

"Good girl, I'll see you in a few hours, Princess."

Angelo placed me on the bed and kiss my head, leaving me flustered and sexually deprived.

What would my reward be?

And most importantly, what lesson did he have in store for me?

I know he's forbidden. Off limits. But I find myself craving his touch. Whether it's gentle or rough. The way he calls me Princess makes me want to be a good girl for him. But... the way he tells me he loves it when I defy him makes me want to be a bad girl.

Oh yes, Daddy.

Spank me.

Punish me.

And after, hold me in your arms and call me a good girl.

His little Princess.

My brother could never know. This would be our little secret. Well... until I find the right time to tell him the truth. That I've started to fall for his boss.

Chapter 5

Angelo

It's a good thing I walked away when I did. Temptation almost got my ass. I was just seconds away from sliding my hand in the front of her pants and finger fucking the hell out of her sweet pussy.

Sweet little Vivianna.

I shook my head and laughed.

She wasn't innocent. Far from it. Such a horny little creature.

"Something funny, boss?" Vito asked.

"Just thinking about all the ways I'm going to torture the bastard spreading lies."

Vito nodded.

"Do you have news for me?"

I was ready to be done with the traitor. Whoever thought they could fuck with Matteo's sister had another thing coming.

"No, not yet. Close though."

"Keep looking, I want this done and soon."

That way I could get Vivianna alone without any distractions. Daddy has big plans for his little Princess. She has no idea what she's unleashed. I'll keep my promise to Matteo. I promised him not to fuck Vivianna.

But… there are other ways to bring her to an orgasm. Daddy's got many ways to bring the Princess to her knees.

I curled my lips at the thought of her tied to my bed.

Thighs spread.

Nipples clamped.

My face buried between her legs.

A quivering mess.

Devouring her sweet pussy.

Or... maybe she'd look better riding my face.

I can't decide.

"Something wrong, boss?" I hear Matteo ask.

Where the hell did he come from?

"Fine, just thinking." I muttered.

Thinking of all the ways I want to defile your sister.

"I need a favor."

I raised a brow.

"I need to take a few days off. It seems Roman is off to his old ways again."

Perfect.

More time alone with Vivianna.

"Of course, take all the time you need."

Matteo narrowed his eyes. "Just like that? No argument or details?"

"Yes, Matteo," I sighed. "Just like that. If you're worried about your sister, rest assured, she'll be just fine. Go deal with Roman and I'll make sure she behaves."

"She's a handful. Are you sure?"

"Go and that's a direct order. I'll make sure she eats properly and goes to bed when she's supposed to."

• •

I stepped into the library after dinner, my dick hard as a rock.

Vivianna, the fucking tease Queen, tortured me throughout the entire dinner. Moaning as she ate her steak. Licking her lips. Dipping her finger into the cup of Ranch dressing and sucked her finger seductively. I couldn't help but imagine her on her knees with my dick inside her mouth.

Like I said, nothing but a damn tease.

Hell, she even slid her foot between my thighs to stroke me through my pants. It's a damn miracle I didn't make a mess in my boxers.

I rounded the corner to see her leaned up against the bookcase. She pouted and purred. "You kept me waiting, Daddy."

Vivianna was pushing it. Teasing. Pushing me to the brink of losing control. Being a bad girl. You know what? I love it. And Daddy? He was itching to give her a lesson. Wanted to show her what happens to naughty little things that tease their Daddy.

"You like being my bad girl, yes?"

"Mmm, maybe. You want to punish me, Daddy?"

"Yes," I growled. "There are so many things I want to do to you. But right now, I want you to turn around. Hands on the bookcase."

"But Daddy, don't you want to play with me?" she wined.

I found her hips and ground my hips against her. "Oh Princess, I do and I am. Now, be a good girl and do as Daddy says."

She widened her eyes when my right hand came down on the front of her thigh.

"Or if you prefer, I can shove you to your knees and punish that dirty mouth with my dick. It's up to you. Spanking or mouth fucked by your brother's boss?"

"I'd rather be fucked by you. Preferably in the ass."

"No, Princess. If I fuck you, it damn sure won't be there. I'll take you in your tight little cunt and make you Daddy's slut. So, either turn around or get ready to bow to your King."

I know I'm about to screw myself, but dammit, Vivianna tempts me way too much. Never had I been so out of control. I wanted to kiss her lips. I wanted to kiss her everywhere. Mouth. Neck. Breasts. Nipples. Belly. Until I was buried between her thighs. Tasting her pussy. Drinking her up.

I crushed my lips against her mouth and groaned. Fuck it. I needed more. So, I took what I wanted. She's the forbidden fruit. I'm the darkness that corrupted Eve's mind.

Did I feel any remorse for betraying Matteo?

No way.

Not when I couldn't pull away.

Because Vivianna tasted way too damn good to stop.

"Please," Vivianna moaned, "Please, don't stop."

I tore away from her mouth and tilted my head to whisper harshly in her ear. "You'll get more when I think you've been punished enough. Now, Princess, turn around and put your hands on the bookcase. Daddy needs to teach his little girl a lesson."

Vivianna turned around, placing her hands on the bookcase. I gave her a swift smack to her right ass cheek. She cried out. I gave her another and smiled cynically. My Princess loves it.

"Oooh, harder."

I palmed her ass and squeezed hard. She arched her back and moaned out my name. She loved that too. My naughty girl likes it rough. Filthy little thing. Maybe a spanking was too easy on her. Maybe I need to get her on the knees and face fuck the girl. Make her suck Daddy's dick like the slut she was.

I twisted her around and pushed her to her knees. "Be a good girl and open wide for Daddy."

Yep, I was a bad, bad man for doing this. But you know what? I couldn't care less. Because my need to feel her had won. The Devil had officially won the war.

Sorry Matteo, but I can't help myself.

Vivianna was just too much of a temptation to fight it.

Chapter 6

Vivianna

Angelo's words sent a shiver down my spine. Lord, help me. This man had me willing to do anything. Me on my knees was proof of that. I was ready and willing to take him in my mouth. Take everything he gave me. Inch by inch. Just to hear him say those two little words.

Good girl.

I opened my mouth as he dropped his pants. Not only was Angelo full of tattoos and muscle, his cock was huge. Bigger than I'd ever seen. Thick. Long. So hard for me.

If my Brother can see me now. I could just see his livid face. He'd have a damn heart attack. Lock me up for the rest of my life. Probably commit murder.

I wrapped my hand around his length, giving him a few stroked. Angelo growled as he grabbed a fistful of my hair. He forced the head between my lips and forced his way into my mouth.

"Good girl. Such a bambina obediente." He groaned.

Angelo cursed under his breath as I massaged his balls. He yanked on my hair, jerking my mouth off his cock. Just when I think he's changed his mind, he thrust back inside my mouth.

"Relax your throat, baby girl. Daddy's going to fuck your mouth now."

His demand made me whimper against him and do as I'm told. He punished my mouth. Fucked me like a dirty slut. And you know what? I liked it. I really, really liked being his dirty girl. He makes me desire him. Brings me pleasure like I've never felt. I don't know why, but I love his dominate side.

"Going to cum now, Princess. Fill that beautiful mouth with Daddy's cum. Swallow it. Every. Fucking. Drop."

I gagged slightly when his thrusts quickened with more force. Angelo dominated me. Used my body. He filled my mouth and I took every drop. Just to be his good girl. All for him.

Angelo helped me off my knees and pressed his forehead against mine. He inhaled sharply and exhaled deeply. It was as if he was fighting the urge to hold himself back. He brushed his lips against mine as I ran my hands down his chest.

"I can't fight it any longer, Vivianna. Princess, are a temptation I can't stay away from."

"Then, don't fight it anymore." I whispered.

"You are mine, Princess. Mine to touch. To kiss. To ravage."

"But?"

"But I can't take your virginity. I won't fuck you out of respect for Matteo."

"You already crossed that bridge when you came in my mouth."

He sighed and pulled away to fix his pants. "I know."

"No, it won't. Matteo will find out and when he does, he'll be ready to spill blood. Mine to be exact."

"Shh, it can be our little secret. Nobody has to find out. Our little secret."

"Fuck, he's going to kill me when he finds out."

Angelo wrapped his arm around my waist and kissed me. It wasn't rough. He was soft. Gentle. Passionate. Just like a Princess should be kissed.

Chapter 7

Angelo

Each night, Vivianna come to me. Sleeps next to me in my bed. She has no idea how bad I want to take her. How hard it is to hold myself back. Thankfully, Matteo is still dealing with his cousin.

Is it bad I want him to stay gone for a while?

Holding sweet little Vivianna feels so good. So right. Like she was always meant to be in my arms. In my bed.

I haven't missed the glares I've received from Vito when he sees us together. If I didn't know any better, I'd say that he's got a little crush on the blonde beauty.

Too bad, Vito.

She's not yours.

But... she's also not mine.

For now though, she is.

Daddy's little Princess.

The thought of her being with another man made my blood boil. Vinnie tells me I'm just jealous. I laughed at the word. I wasn't jealous. I'm territorial. There's a difference. Being jealous would mean she's not mine. Being territorial is being protective and possessive over what already belongs to me.

I haven't taken Vivianna's virginity. Not yet. However, I have brought her to her knees in other ways. Like making her cum on my tongue. I've also given back to her and came in her mouth. But if she's a bad girl, I won't hesitate to put her over my knee. Give Daddy's little girl a firm hand.

"Vivianna," I warned. "I don't think you want to tease me right now. Not in front of company."

"But Daddy..." She whined, sliding her hand up my inner thigh.

I leaned over and whispered harshly in her ear. "Don't tease me, baby girl. Do you want me to take you over my knee and spank that pretty little ass until it glows?"

"Then... what are you waiting for? Spank me, Daddy."

My head snapped up and glanced across the table, demanding Carmella and Vinnie. "Everyone out. Now!"

I scooted my chair back and took her chin between my finger and thumb, forcing her head to the side. "Bring me a wooden spoon, Princess."

"What?" Vivianna whispered.

"You heard me, baby girl. Go fetch a wooden spoon and bend over my knee."

"Yes, Daddy."

My dick was hard. I have a feeling I would need to take this to my bedroom. But fuck it. She wants to tease. Fine. I'll show her what bad little things get when they tempt the big bad wolf.

I licked my lips as she walked across the room. The sway of her hips had me on edge. The things I wanted to do to her. Vivianna returned, spoon in hand. I didn't miss the excitement dancing in her blue eyes. I took the spoon from her and patted my thigh. "Bend over, Princess."

Vivianna bent over, looking over her shoulder. I lifted her dress over her ass and ran the spoon over her bare ass.

"No panties. Were you looking to get spanked?" I growled.

"Ang..."

Smack!

"Daddy! My name is Daddy to you, little girl."

"Mmm, Daddy. Spank me harder!" She moaned, grinding against my hardened member.

I spanked her again. And again. Harder with each time. Until her ass was thoroughly marked. She arched her back and ground her hips.

"Who's Daddy's bad girl?" I asked.

"I am, Daddy."

I pulled her off my knee and set her on my lap. She straddled me and pressed against my cock. All it would take is one second to free my cock and take her right here. But it would be too risky. Anyone could walk in. The only ones that knew what I was doing with Vivianna was Carmella, Vinnie, and us two. Matteo had no idea the perverted thoughts I had about his sister.

"Keep it up and you'll get another punishment for teasing me."

"I like teasing, Daddy."

"What the hell is going on?!" Vito growled.

"Fuck." I swore. "Not now, Vito."

"She's just a kid! Seventeen, Angelo."

"Go up to my room and wait for me. You don't want to see this." I whispered and kissed her forehead.

I waited until she left the room and glared at Vito. "What's it to you?"

Vito scowled. "What if I had been Matteo? Huh? I bet he'd love to walk in on his boss and sister practically fucking."

"You're not to say anything. Not a goddamn thing." I hissed.

"Yeah, whatever you say, boss." I didn't miss the disgust when he said the last word.

"You're supposed to be at the club. Why are you back?"

"For your information, I caught wind of old man Romanov's plans."

"And?"

"And his plan is to take you out."

I scoffed.

"Let me be more specific. His plan is to go after the one thing that matters to you the most. Your weakness."

"I don't have a weakness. Nothing will break me."

Vito tapped his temple. "Think real hard. What is the one thing you care about right now?"

Fuck!

Vivianna.

"Triple the security. No one comes in unless it's Matteo. Nobody leaves either."

"And for the record, I don't like Vivianna. She's a brat."

I grinned. "I know."

I wouldn't let anything happen to her. Nobody would dare take her away. I wouldn't let them.

With a single nod, he leaves me to my thoughts.

How the hell did anyone know about Vivianna?

Unless…

There's a rat.

I know Vinnie and Carmella would never betray me.

So, who was it?

I turned to see Vivianna in the doorway. Hopefully, she didn't hear anything.

"Is everything okay?"

I swallowed hard and lied. "Everything is fine. Let's get you up to your room."

It wasn't fine, but she didn't need to know that. The less she knew, the safer she would be. She didn't need to know what kind of danger I put her in. Not yet.

I led her up to her room, making sure to lock the door. I didn't want any interruptions for what I had planned. I wanted to taste her on my tongue. Ravage her sweetness. Forget about everything.

"Get on the bed, Princess. Daddy wants to taste you. Make you cum in my mouth."

Chapter 8

Vivianna

I laid back on the bed and parted my thighs. Angelo crawled onto the bed in a slow and predatory slither. Like a snake about to go in for the kill. His hands skimmed my thighs as he tortured me with his mouth.

"Please, Daddy." I begged.

"Patience, little girl." He growled.

A soft moan escaped my lips when he buried his face between my thighs.

This was wrong.

But at the same time, it felt so right.

So good.

Angelo flicked his tongue against my clit and thrust his finger inside. My hips ground against him, my back arching. I was desperate for him. Wanted him to dominate.

"God, yes!" I cried.

Angelo licked and sucked. Making his Princess feel pleasure. He pumped his fingers at a steady pace. Not to fast. Not to slow. Just enough drive me crazy.

"I'm going to cum, Daddy!"

"No!" Angelo growled. "Not until Daddy says so, baby girl."

"Please," I mewled. "I need to cum."

My plea only drove Angelo to pump his finger more aggressively. My eyelids fluttered as I threaded my fingers through his hair. Just when I was on the verge of my release, he growled low and dangerously. "Cum for Daddy."

And I do.

The dam breaks.

I came the harder than I ever had before.

Angelo slid up my body and kissed me gently, muttering against my mouth. "So beautiful."

"Thank you, Daddy."

"Anything for you, baby girl."

The next few days, Angelo and I fell into a rhythm. He kept me close. Protected me with his life. Cared for me. I came to him at night. I slept in his arms. Something about him made me feel safe.

My brother was still gone and that's okay. That meant more time alone with Angelo.

"What do you want to do today, Princess?" Angelo whispered as he stroked my hair.

"I want..." I swallowed hard. "I want Daddy to fuck me. Fuck me like a dirty girl."

"Fuck, I can't. You know I can't. Matteo..."

"Isn't here. I can fuck whoever I want."

"I won't take your virginity."

"Who said I was a virgin?"

"Who was it?!"

Angelo pinned me to the bed, his eyes dark and dangerous. He curled his fingers around my neck and squeezed. I gasped when he whispered harshly in my ear. "Tell me who I have to fucking kill, Princess."

"Ang... elo." I moaned.

"Tell me who did it."

"I… it was just a guy."

He narrowed his eyes and hissed. "A dead fucking guy. Give me a name."

I loved how jealous he got. That's one thing I loved about him.

Angelo pulled back and raised a brow. "Name. Now."

"I can't." I whispered.

"Tell me or I'll comb the city until I find the bastard."

"You can't kill him."

"And why is that?"

I took a breath and whispered. "Because Matteo already did."

I remembered that night. I just spent the night with my boyfriend. We had the best night. Long story short, he mysteriously died. I wasn't stupid. I knew my brother killed him. I couldn't prove it. The next day, I saw it on the news. I didn't love the guy, but he didn't deserve that. Not because he had sex with me.

"Fuck, Princess." Angelo whispered, loosening his grip on my neck. "I hurt you."

"It's okay. I like it when you're rough. I might be a Princess, but I'm not a fragile Princess."

Knock. Knock.

I covered my mouth and widened my eyes. I heard the knock again. Angelo pressed his finger to his lips. He covered me up and went to the door. I could hear Vinnie at the door.

"Matteo called. He said he won't be back for a while."

"What happened?"

"It seems Roman is being taken to rehab. Matteo says he'll be back in a few weeks."

"That's fine."

I heard the door shut. I turned over on my side and beckoned him with my finger. He locked the door and pounced on me. He crushed his lips against mine and growled in my mouth. "Fuck, baby girl."

No matter how much he touched me, I craved him even more. Every touch made me hungry for more. And when he manhandled me? I loved it.

He pulled away from the kiss and whispered. "I hate to leave you, but I have to go to the club. Need to make sure everything is running smoothly."

"Daddy," I whined. "I don't want you to go."

He kissed me again. "I'll be back before you know it, baby girl. I'll have Vinnie and Carmella stay with you."

"No Vito?"

"No. Go get dressed and go down for lunch. I'll be back within the hour."

I didn't want him to go, but I guess the boss does actually have to do work. I wrapped my arms around him and kissed him. He deepened the kiss, pulling me against him.

"You can always take me with you." I suggested.

"A club is no place for you. Besides, Matteo would kill me if I allowed you to go with me on business."

"He'd also kill you for this, but that didn't stop you, did it?"

He curved his lips and nodded. "This is different. Here, you're safe. In the club, anyone could take you."

"You would protect me, Daddy." I kissed him again.

"You, Princess, are a fucking tease. You make it so hard to leave right now." He groaned.

"Stay." I urged. "Show me what happens to bad girls that tease Daddy."

Angelo palmed my ass and ground his hips against mine.

"Patience, little girl. When I get back, I'll do just that."

Angelo kissed me one last time before getting dressed in a different suit to leave me with Vinnie and Carmella. Fifteen minutes later, I'm walking down to the kitchen when I hear a crash. I froze, not sure what to do.

"Vinnie? Carmella?" I say.

I take another step and peek around the corner. I see Vinnie and Carmella tied to a chair. Both fear in their eyes. Not their fear. Fear for me.

"Run, get out of here!" Vinnie whisper yells.

"I can't leave you." I whispered.

"Go, sweetie. Vinnie and I will be fine." Carmella whispered back to me.

I turn to leave, but I'm faced with someone I've never seen before. From the looks of it, it's not one of Angelo's men, and he's not friendly. I turn to leave, but he yanks me back by the hips and covers my mouth.

"He'll kill you for this!" Vinnie growls.

"Oh yeah, does Matteo know his boss is hittin' his sister's pussy?"

Vinnie clenched his jaw, fighting to break free.

"Don't worry, tell Angelo my boss will make sure to keep it nice and warm for him." The man says.

"Fuck you, you do this and you're dead. All. Of. You." Carmella screams. "Fucking dead!"

The last thing I see is Vinnie and Carmella's face as I fall into darkness.

Chapter 9

Angelo

I hated leaving her behind. I wanted nothing but to bring her with me. But I knew the risks. One being Matteo had no idea about how close I'd gotten to his sister. The other… it was too dangerous for her to be seen with me. I had enemies. And whoever was trying to get to me, they knew it.

"Boss?" John, the manager asked. "Is something wrong?"

"No, I just wanted to make sure everything is going smoothly while Matteo is away on business."

"Everything is fine." He assured me.

I raised a brow. "Are you sure? You look like you're about to blow a gasket."

"I'm… fine."

"No, you're not. What gives?"

"It's Bailey. She's driving me crazy."

"Refresh my memory. Who is Bailey?"

I pinched the bridge of his nose and took a deep breath. "She's my daughter's best friend. How do you do it, boss?"

"I'm sorry, but what do you mean?"

"How do you fight temptation?"

"Very carefully. Very fucking carefully."

"She tests me and… fuck me, she teases me."

Vito meets my gaze and swallowed hard as he's talking on his phone. I narrow my eyes at him and excuse myself from John. When I get to Vito, dread fills me. Whatever he was told isn't good. And nothing could prepare me for his next words.

"It's Vivianna... she's been taken."

Nothing in the world could have prepared me for this. Fuck! Why didn't I just bring her with me?

"Tell me you're joking. Tell me this is one of Vivianna's pranks."

Vito averts his gaze and shakes his head.

"Vinnie? Carmella?"

"Unharmed. They only came for Miss Vivianna."

I was supposed to protect her. Fuck. I couldn't even do that. And God, what about Matteo? Roman? How do I tell my second-in-command I failed to keep her safe. I told him I would.

"I'll find her, boss." Vito whispered.

"Vito, I..."

"I'll assemble a team and find her. Matteo never has to know."

He's covering for me?

"What's your play, Vito?"

"It... should've been me. Tanya..."

I grabbed him by the collar. "What the fuck about her?! You're not married to the cunt anymore. Why should it have been you?"

"I... Tanya had someone put a bug in Vivianna's room. The leak has been taken care of. Now, let me fix this. Let me make up for it."

"Fine, but it she dies, it's your life. Do you understand?"

"Yes, boss."

"Go! And make sure you don't go alone."

I released him and felt my entire world crashing down. I pressed a hand to my chest and closed my eyes. My emotions were all over the place. I wanted to kill Vito's ex-wife. And at the same time, I wanted to cry for the first time in my life. I haven't felt this sad since my mother died. Since my father murdered her. And now, the question is, how do I keep something like this from Matteo. Because if he finds out, he'll know about what I've been doing with his sister. That I betrayed him. I wasn't ready to give Vivianna up just yet. I'll be damned it I lose her to a whore like Tanya. Vivianna meant too much to me.

Shit!

Did I really just say that?

That she meant too much to me.

By the time I got back to the estate, my heart was in pieces. All I could think about was her. I'd been so wrapped up in Vivianna to see what was going on right under my nose. I stepped into the estate. Nobody dared look at me. They knew better. Not when I was so angry. The more I thought about it, the angrier I got. Most of all, I was angry at myself.

"Angelo," I heard Carmella whisper.

I ignored her and walked into my office. I would get her back and I would never let the girl out of my sight again. I stood in front of my safe and punched in the code. It beeped and I opened it, retrieving my mother's gun. I tucked it in the pocket of my jacket and turned to see Carmella. She was giving me sympathetic expression. Like she was saying, I'm sorry. She was acting as if she was already dead. She handed me a glass of whiskey, which I took immediately. I downed the contents and handed it back to her. She placed it on my desk and sighed.

"I'm sorry." Carmella whispered.

I held my hand up and shook my head. "She's not dead yet. She's not. I'm…"

"Angelo, this is all my fault. I should've… fuck, I should've known something wasn't right with Damon. He…" Carmella trailed off.

"Damon?! He's the one who took her?"

Carmella's nod is all it takes to storm past her. I couldn't believe someone I trusted was the one after me.

"Wait, where are you going?" She exclaimed.

I turned and narrowed my eyes. "I'm going to get her back. And after, I'm going to kill each and every last one of the fuckers. They're going to pay for taking her. For hurting her. And if they touched her, I'll fucking castrate the motherfuckers."

"I'll go with you." Carmella murmured.

"Wait a minute. I told Vito to…"

"Vito to what?"

"He told me… fuck… where's Vinnie?"

Carmella grabbed my wrist and pulled me in for a hug. Sure, me and Carmella have fucked. But that's all it was. Just a release. She knew what it was. But truth be told, fucking was all it was. I haven't touch Carmella since I've been with Vivianna. I closed my eyes and all I could see was Vivianna. The one who has somehow stolen my heart. I could feel tears threatening to spill, but I held them back. I was the Boss. I couldn't let anyone know my true feelings for Matteo's sister.

"Vinnie and Vito have gone to rescue her. They'll bring back your girl and all will be fine." Carmella whispered.

"I think… I think I'm falling in love with her. That's why when I get her back, I'm going to let her go. I can't… I wouldn't be able to live with myself if something happened to her."

"Angelo, love finds you, you don't find it. What you and Vivianna have, it's meant to be."

"Matteo will kill me. I promised him."

"Oh my God, have you slept with her?"

"No, yes, kind of."

Carmella furrowed her brows. "Either you have or you haven't."

"I haven't fucked her. She sleeps in my bed and I've done other things, but... no, I haven't fucked her yet."

"You're in love with her." She mused. "I should've known when you haven't asked for me for days."

I clenched my jaw and pulled away from her. "I care for her."

"I'm sorry." Carmella told me.

"It wasn't your fault."

"No, I'm sorry but I can't let you leave. I was given strict orders not to let you leave and for that I'm sorry."

"I don't..." I slurred, my vision blurred.

"I'm sorry, but I can't let you leave. If something..."

I braced myself against the wall. "What the fuck did you do to me?!"

I'm sorry is all I hear before darkness takes over me.

Chapter 10

Vivianna

"He will k-kill you for this." I managed through choked sobs.

His hot breaths hit my neck as he thrust into me. I felt sick each time he kissed my neck. His breath was foul. Putrid. I was powerless to him as he continued to assault me.

"Fuck, so tight." He grunted in my ear.

I squeezed my eyes shut and prayed that Angelo was on his way. Anybody. My wrists and ankles were tied to the bedpost. Each thrust was like a knife to the chest. I couldn't breathe. So hard to breathe.

"Do you know who I am?" I cried out. "He's going to kill you."

The man chuckled in my ear and hissed. "Angelo won't even be able to recognize you after this. And Matteo, he'll be far to broken to try to come after me."

He pulled out and spit on my face. "Worthless Italian slut."

My chest heaved, my sobs filling the room. I closed my eyes and prayed again. Prayed for Angelo. Vito. Anyone to take me away from this hell. People may think Angelo is the Devil, but no, the real monsters were here with me. If anything, Angelo was my Dark Prince.

"Please hurry, Angelo." I whispered, weakening by the second.

When I opened my eyes, I was met with a pair of sinister eyes. It was a woman. She gripped my chin and growled. "All of this could've been avoided if only Vito hadn't pissed me off."

"Please, let me go." I whispered.

"Not yet, not until I get what I want." She says with a scowl.

"W-what do you want?" I choked out.

"My husband to join the right side."

"Husband?"

"Oh, silly girl, Vito is my ex-husband."

"Angelo and my brother will come for you."

"Silly girl, do you think Angelo actually cares about you. You are nothing but a challenge because Matteo warned him off you."

"You're lying. He… cares about me."

"Has he fucked you yet?" She asked, raising a brow.

"No." I whispered.

That's not right. He cares about me. I know he does. Calls me his Princess.

"Tanya, they're here." A voice yells.

"Be a dear and tell Angelo and his goons I said hello. And if he asks, Simon had a real good time keeping your pussy warm."

"Please, don't' leave me like this! Please…" But it's too late. She's gone.

I closed my eyes, suddenly exhausted. I hear the door slam open and fear grips me. no. Not again. My eyelids flutter to see a familiar face. Vito takes a knife and curses under his breath. I let out a whimper as each limb is released from the rope.

"Fuck, what did they do to you?" He whispered.

"Help me, please."

He takes off his jacket and helps me sit up. Vito gathers me in his arms and carried me out the door. He meets Vinnie and passes me to him. "Get her out of her. I'll hold them off."

"But..." Vinnie says.

"Go, Vinnie. Just get her back home safely."

"But Angelo..." He hissed.

"Go! This is my mess, I'll clean it up. Miss Vivianna, I'm sorry."

Vinnie carried me through the warehouse and thrust me into the SUV. He buckled my belt and ran to the other side. I glanced out the window to see Vito being shoved into a van.

"Vinnie, Vito..."

He started the vehicle and shook his head. "He'll be fine."

"He saved me." I whispered. "We can't just leave him."

Vinnie peeled out and drove away. When he pulled out on the highway, he glanced at me. "Vivianna, did they..."

I know what he was about to say, so I pressed my cheek against the glass and said. "I don't' want to talk about it. Please, you can't tell him. He'll be so mad at me."

"Your brother?"

I shook my head. "No, not my brother. You can't tell Angelo."

I tried to close my eyes, but all I could see was that horrid man. The Russian asshole who forced himself on me. Vinnie grabbed my hand and whispered. "Your brother doesn't know yet. And Angelo, he cares about you."

I wiped a tear and asked. "If he cares so much, why didn't he come for me?"

"Because Vito and I knew he would go on a warpath to find you."

"Where is he?"

"I had him drugged, so he wouldn't leave the estate."

I sighed and eventually closed my eyes, letting sleep take over. The next time I woke up, I was back in my room. Carmella sat on the bed and placed a glass of water and two pills.

"Hey, how are you feeling?"

I forced a smile. "Tired, hungry, thirsty. I feel like I got ran over by a truck."

"That's to be expected. All things considered."

"Where's Angelo?"

"He's still out. You know, he loves you."

"He what?"

She tucked a strand of my hair behind my ear and nodded "I've never seen him so angry when you disappeared. He was so angry at himself."

"It wasn't his fault."

"He blames himself because he couldn't protect you. Promise me you won't push him away."

"What about Matteo?"

"He'll get over it. I'll go fetch you some food. What would you like?"

"A sandwich will do. Nothing too heavy."

"I'll be right back. I'm glad you're okay."

Would I be able to come back from this?

Could I heal from the wounds I endured?

I'd like to think so. As long as I had Angelo, I would be fine.

But my brother? He was going to be ready to spill blood when he finds out. I slid out of bed and sighed, walking to the bathroom. I glanced at my reflection and felt tears threatening to spill. My face was bruised and my bottom lip was split. I closed my eyes and silently sobbed. How could someone do that to a woman? Why? When I opened my eyes, I didn't even recognize myself. Angelo wouldn't want me like this. Broken. Damaged. Used.

"Vivianna?" I heard Carmella call out to me.

That's when I let out a scream and braced myself against the sink. How do I go on as everything is normal. What was once the lively girl was nothing but a shattered Princess. I hated feeling this way. Hated the fact I couldn't fight the bastard.

"Vivianna, I've brought…"

"I hate him! I fucking hate the bastard." I cried out.

Carmella wrapped her arms around me and whispered softly. "Shh, I got you."

"I want Daddy!"

"Your Daddy? But he's dead."

"No, I want Angelo. He's the only one that can make it all go away."

"Oh, you mean you… ok, I'll go get Angelo. Will you be okay while I go get him?"

"Yes." I whispered.

"Okay, I'll have Vinnie go get him for you."

Chapter 11

Angelo

I groaned as I opened my eyes. I sat up and held my head in my hands. My head throbbed terribly. I furrowed my eyebrows, trying to figure out what happened. Vinnie cleared his throat. "You're awake."

Oh, yeah.

I remember.

I was drugged.

Vivianna was kidnapped.

And me?

I was pissed.

"Yeah, no thanks to you, dick." I growled.

"She's safe, but there is a problem. A few of them actually."

"What is it?"

Vinnie sighed. "Vito… they took him. And Vivianna… she needs you more than ever."

"What's that supposed to mean?"

"She… Simon… look, there's no easy way to say this."

"Fucking spit it out!" I bellowed.

"He did things to her… terrible things." He whispered.

"Jesus, don't tell me he…" I swallowed hard. "Tell me it's not true."

"I'm sorry, Angelo. I'm so damn sorry."

"Get a team and go bring Vito back. I've got to go see Vivianna."

He placed his hand on my shoulder as I stood up. "Take care of her. She's been through a lot."

My throat went dry at the thought of what shape my Princess would be in. It broke my heart to think she suffered because of me. If only I'd taken her with me. And I'd yet to call Matteo to break the news. He would definitely want revenge. I stood outside her door and placed my hand on the door. I grabbed the doorknob and swallowed hard. When I entered the room, my entire world came crashing down.

Vivianna was curled up on the bed. Battered. Bruised. Broken.

"Angelo, I need you." She whispered as she looked up at me.

"I'm sorry, Princess. I'm so goddamn sorry this happened."

I sat down on the bed and gathered her in my arms. She clung to me, silently sobbing in my chest. I never knew love could hurt this much. The sight of Vivianna in pain made my chest ache.

"I've got you, Princess. Daddy's here." I whispered, kissing the top of her head.

"Don't ever let me go."

"Shh, it's okay. I'm here."

The more I tried to calm her, the more she cried in my arms. I couldn't do anything. Not a damn thing to comfort her. For the first time in my life, I was powerless. I knew one thing. I was going to avenge her.

"I have to tell Matteo what happened." I told her softly.

"No."

I sighed. "He needs to know what happened."

"He's going to be so mad at me."

"He won't be mad at you. Just the bastard that hurt you."

"Will you lay with me?" She asked.

"I will be here when you wake up. Just close your eyes, Princess."

I stroked her hair and closed my eyes. If I could take her pain away, I would. But I couldn't. That's what hurt the most. The door opened and Carmella carried a tray, placing it on the nightstand. "She was asking for you. I didn't know what to do."

"It's fine."

"I'm sorry about earlier." Carmella whispered.

"It's fine. All that matters is she's home safely."

"Matteo called."

"You didn't..."

"No, I just didn't have the heart to tell him. Nobody should ever go through that."

Vivianna finally falls asleep in my arms. I hear the door open, expecting to see Vinnie or Carmella. I don't. Instead, I'm faced with Matteo's murderous glare. He eyes his sister in my arms. I press a finger to my lips and nod to the door. I gently lay her down and cover her up. When I meet Matteo outside the door, he shoots me a glare.

"It wasn't..."

"What happened? I thought you said she was safe." He whispered.

"I went to the club. She was safe when I left her here. So I thought."

"I'll fucking kill him."

"It was Simon. He..." I couldn't bear to finish it. Because if I did, it would be too real. Too painful. And I didn't need to let Matteo know I'd started to fall for his sister.

Matteo's head drops and closes his eyes. "Did he... did he touch her?"

"I'm sorry. I'm so fucking sorry. If only I'd taken her with me. Maybe... fuck..."

"I'll. Kill. Him." He says, venom dripping from each word.

We couldn't go after them yet. Not when Vito was still in their clutches. I didn't even want to know what he was going through right now. Probably being tortured by his cunt of an ex.

"We can't go after them yet."

"Why? He fucking raped her!" Matteo growled, frustration in his voice.

"Vinnie and Vito rescued her. Vito, he sacrificed himself to save her. He risked his life for her."

"What?"

"I know you don't get along with Vito, but he saved her life and stayed behind. Just so Vinnie could bring her home."

Vivianna's scream echoes through the estate. Matteo goes to run after her, but I stop him. "She's not going to be the same. Let me help her. Go get some sleeping pills from my office. I'll take care of her."

"You better keep your hands to yourself. I mean it."

"Please, just let me help her. I'm the only one she'll let get close to her. She's... afraid you'll be angry with her."

He scoffed. "She's my sister. I have a right to see her."

"Let me rephrase that. She's scared right now."

His face falls. "She's afraid of me."

For the first time, I see my second-in-command in pain. He can't stand the thought of his own blood cower down from him in fear. His own sister is afraid of him.

"Just give her some time." I offer him a smile.

"I'll be right back. Make sure she knows I'm not mad at her."

"I will. And Matteo, she will be okay."

I step into the room and see Vivianna sitting up. She's rocking back and forth, tears streaming down her face. I sit down next to her and wrap my arms around her, whispering in her ear. "Daddy's here."

"Angelo, make I stop." She whimpered.

"Shh, just relax. Matteo knows and wanted me to tell you he's not angry with you. Only upset that someone touched you. Don't be afraid."

"I'm not afraid."

"Then, why do you not want to see him?"

"Because I feel so ashamed."

Matteo steps into the room and spares her a glance. He sets the water and pills on the nightstand and leans in to whisper to me. "Please, take care of her. I may have already lost my cousin, I can't lose her."

I nod.

I can't help but feel guilty for betraying him. Not only had I touched his sister, I've also fallen in love with her. I handed Vivianna the glass of water and slipped it into her hand. I reached over and grabbed the pills, giving her two. "Take this. It will make you relax."

It doesn't take Vivianna long to fall back to sleep. I settle in bed and hold her in my arms. I have to admit, it feels good to have her in my arms. I'll never let her out of my sight again. And if I have to take her to the club, so be it.

Chapter 12

Vivianna

Something about Angelo brings me peace. I wake up to his strong arms wrapped protectively around my waist. His face is pressed into my neck, his hot breath fans my skin. I wiggle against him, only for him to groan in my ear. "Stop moving, baby girl."

"Daddy..."

This seems to only make him hold onto me tighter. Angelo loosens his grip on me and to my disappointment he pulls away. I feel panic rise as he sits up to put some distance between us.

"Don't leave me, Daddy." I whispered.

"Vivianna, he's back. Your brother is back and wants to see you."

I shoot up in bed and widen my eyes.

Did Matteo catch us together?

Is that why Angelo is so distant?

Angelo holds his head in his hands and murmurs. "We have to put some distance between us, baby girl. If he... if he suspects anything, it will end badly."

"Are you breaking up with me?"

He raises his head and shakes his head. "No, but we have to be careful now that he's back. Do you understand that?"

I hugged him from the back and kissed his cheek. "I understand, Daddy."

"Which means you can't call me Daddy in front of him. We have to be cautious now." Angelo tells me.

"Can you kiss me?"

Angelo eyes the door and twists around to cup my face. He brushes his lips against mine to capture my mouth. His kiss is gentle, careful not to hurt me. I deepen the kiss, but he pulls away. "We have to stop or I don't think I'll be able to if this keeps going. I want to do so many things to you. So. Many. Dirty. Things."

"Will I be able to sleep with you tonight? I can't be alone at night, Daddy."

"I'll see what I can do. Are you ready to see Matteo?"

"I... you promise he's not mad at me?"

He pecks my lips and whispers. "The only one he's mad at is the bastards who hurt you. Same goes for me."

"I'm ready to see him."

"I put you some clothes in the bathroom. Change and I'll send Matteo in."

"Thank you for staying with me when I was scared, Daddy."

"Anything for you, baby girl."

I dressed in the shirt and sweats. They were a few sizes too big on me. That's okay. As long as I'm fully covering the bruises on my body. Well, except for my wrists and face. I stepped out of the bathroom to see Matteo sitting at the edge of my bed. He's not in a suit, which is unusual for him. He always wears one. He meets my gaze and clenches his jaw when he sees the bruises on my face.

"What did they do to you, baby sister?"

"I'm okay now." I assured him.

That was a lie. I wasn't okay. He stood and pulled me in for a hug. I've never seen him this way. Weak. Vulnerable. Sad. This wasn't the Matteo I was used to seeing. I wrapped my arms around his waist and whispered. "I'm okay now. I'm safe now."

"Fuck, I thought... when I heard the news... I'm so fucking sorry I left you alone."

"So, you're not mad at me?" I asked.

He pulled back and shook his head. "Not at you. Simon is going to pay for ever laying a hand on you."

"I'll be okay, Matteo."

"You're sure?"

"I think so."

It's been a few days since Matteo's been back, and he's been more protective of me. Angelo and I have barely gotten any time alone. The sexual tension is so thick between Angelo and myself. When Matteo isn't paying attention, I tease Angelo. Just last night, I asked for a chocolate ice cream cone. I slowly licked and sucked the dessert. Angelo looked as if he was about to blow a gasket. Matteo had no idea. But Carmella? She knew and thought it was funny. Vito was brought in late last night. I'd yet to see him, but according to Carmella, it wasn't good. They tortured him for information.

"I want to see Vito and thank him for saving my life." I tell Angelo.

"I'll tell him."

I sighed and rolled my eyes. "I can tell him myself."

I knew he was only being jealous and possessive, but it was what it was.

It was only Angelo and myself at the pool. He was fully dressed, but I was in a one-piece bathing suit. I still wasn't ready to show the scars I received. I stepped out of the pool and wrapped a towel around me. I plopped down in a chair next to Angelo and whispered. "Where's my brother?"

"He's gone to check on Roman. Apparently, there was an incident at the rehab he sent him to."

"So, we're all alone, Daddy?"

"Vivianna," Angelo warned. "You know what that word does, yes?"

"Of course, Daddy."

I knew what teasing him got me. Angelo placed one hand on my thigh and sighed. "We can't. Not out in the open. There are cameras."

"I'm not going to break, Angelo. I've had time to heal."

"You're not ready for that, baby girl. Not for the things Daddy wants to do to you."

His words send tingles through me, a desire for him to do those erotic things to me. I clenched my thighs together as he gave me a firm squeeze. "What things?"

"I want to take you to my office. Spread you out on my desk. Rip this fucking towel off your body and strip you bare. I want spread these thighs and bury my face so deep between them. Eat you up. Make you cum so hard your thighs quiver. But most of all, I want to slide my dick inside you and make sweet love to you."

"Do it. Fuck me, Daddy." I did want him to do those things. But there was something in the way. The one thing preventing him from giving in. My brother.

I reached over and placed my hand between his legs. I could feel how hard he was. Sure, he's brought me to an orgasm with his mouth and fingers, but yet to fuck me the way I wanted him to. Maybe if I weren't the sister of Matteo, he would take me.

"Fuck, you make it so hard to be a gentleman. I'd love nothing but to do good on my promise. But then, I would be breaking my promise to your brother. I'm sorry, but I can't."

"Please, Daddy. I need you."

Chapter 13

Angelo

Vivianna wanted me badly. I was barely holding onto my sanity when she teased me like that. She knew it. My dick throbbed as she stroked me through my pants. It would be so easy to take her to my room.

Matteo's not here.

He would never know, right?

I closed my eyes and took a deep breath as she teased my cock. I opened my eyes to see Vinnie standing on the other side of the pool. He grinned and shook his head. I took Vivianna's wrist and pulled her hand away. If Vinnie could sneak up on my, then Matteo could as well. Vito was currently on bed rest. I relayed the message to him that Vivianna wanted me to tell him. I could see it in his eyes as I told him thank you from her. Regret and anger swirled in his eyes. He felt like it was his fault. But it wasn't. His was a crazy fucking bitch. She would've done something even if he had agreed.

"Go get dressed." I whispered to Vivianna.

"Why? I thought you like my bathing suit."

"I do. That's why you need to change. It makes me think very bad things."

"What about when I do this?"

Vivianna spread her thighs and raised the towel, exposing her skin. Fuck me. She would definitely be getting a spanking later for that. She says she's okay, but I know better. Simon really fucked her up. Badly. She acted wilder than before. And that's bad. Because she was already a wild one.

"Don't make me take you inside and spank you, baby girl."

"But Angelo..."

"Go get dressed and meet me in the theater. I have a surprise for you."

She sucked her bottom lip. "But Daddy, I want to play."

I gave her thigh a smack and threw her a smirk. "You want to play games with me, little girl?"

She nodded.

"You want Daddy to play with you? Fine, but don't say I didn't warn you. Meet me in my bedroom in ten minutes."

I looked at Vinnie again, then back to Vivianna. The things I was going to do to her. So many things. Gag her. Strip her. Tie her to my bed and torture her with my tongue. Pinch her nipples. Mark her with my hand.

"What if I'm not on time?"

"You would like that, wouldn't you? To be a bad girl. Just so I can punish you."

"I like being naughty, Daddy." She whispered.

"That's it, baby girl. Get those punishments racked up for Daddy."

Vivianna stood up and turned to leave, earning her a smack from me. She gasped and ran off. She acts like she didn't like it, but I knew better. She loves it when I spank the defiance out of her.

I stepped into my room and stripped down to my pants. I can't wait until she gets here. I have so many things I want to do to her. I licked my lips and patted my dick. "Down boy."

I opened my dresser and pulled out a few toys. She wants to play? That's fine. Daddy wants to play too. I smirked at the few toys I pulled from the dresser. Nipple clamps. Ball gag. And my personal favorite... feather crop. I grabbed them and set them on my bed.

I glanced at the clock and hissed under my breath. "Rack them points, baby girl. Daddy's going to make you pay when you get here."

Knock. Knock.

I answered it to be met with Vivianna's deep blues. I yanked her into my room, closing the door. I locked it and pushed her against the wall. "You're late."

"I'm sorry, Daddy." She whispered.

"No," I chuckled. "I know you're not sorry. But that's okay, Daddy will remind you what happens to naughty little brats. Strip and lie down on the bed."

Vivianna pulled her bathing suit down her chest, never leaving my eyes. Her nipples hardened as she leaned over to pull it the rest of the way. Like a good girl, she laid back on the bed. She spread her thighs, giving me a perfect view of her pussy. She was wet. Glistening. I walked towards her and picked up the nipple clamps and showed them to her.

"Daddy..."

"Quiet!" I hissed. "It's punishment time, baby girl."

She widened her eyes as I straddled her thighs. With one hand I cupped her breast and leaned down to suck on it. I took it between my teeth and flicked it with my tongue. I released it with a pop and attached the nipple clamp. I tugged, causing her to whimper. Next I did the same with her other nipple. I leaned back and flicked each tight bud with my finger.

"Oooh, Daddy." She moaned.

Next I picked up the ball gag and said. "Open your mouth. I can't have anyone hear your cries when I'm punishing you. Especially not Matteo."

She opened her mouth, causing me to imagine her lips wrapped around my dick. I placed it in her mouth and demanded. "Raise your head."

She obeyed and I fastened it at the back of her head. I cupped her cheek and brush, running my thumb over her bottom lip. "Beautiful. Absolutely fucking stunning like this, baby girl."

I grabbed each wrist and held them above her head. She bucked her hips as I curved my lips into a smirk. "Stay just like this."

I got off the bed and grabbed the crop. She moaned through the gag as I tapped the crop against each nipple a few times. I ran the feather across her nipples and without warning brought in down on her right nipple. She cried out through the gag as I repeated my movements to the other one. My dick twitched as her chest heaved. Still, yet, she never moved from her spot.

"Such a good girl. Do you wish to cum?"

She nodded, not being able to talk through the gag.

"No, you will take your punishment like a good girl. Then, if I allow it, I'll make you cum on Daddy's fingers."

I grabbed her hips and turned her over. She raised up on her hands and knees, spreading her thighs. She arched her back and glanced over her shoulder. I set the crop down and unbuckled my belt. I pulled it out of the loops and folded it in half. "Remember, if it gets to be too much, raise your hand to signal me to stop."

"Mhmm." She moaned.

I knew Matteo wouldn't be back until tonight. It's a four-hour drive to the rehab. Which gives me plenty of time to punish my little Princess. Then after, I'll give her a reward for taking it like a good girl. Of course, she doesn't know that. Another part of her punishment.

Chapter 14

Vivianna

Angelo shot me a wicked grin as I winced when I sat down at the table. No one seemed to notice. Thank goodness for that.

Angelo and I have been sneaking around for weeks now. My brother hasn't taken notice. Maybe he's been too occupied with Roman. Or maybe he's got himself a lady friend.

Who knows what goes on inside his head?

Don't know.

Don't care.

I glanced over at my brother to see him glaring at Angelo.

"Problem, Matteo?" Angelo asked.

"No, boss." Matteo hissed.

I didn't miss the malice in my brother's voice when the word "boss" rolled off his tongue.

"Calm down." I whispered.

"Got something you need to say?" Did my brother know about us?

"Matteo, you need to calm down." Angelo murmured.

"Fuck you," Matteo glared at me. "And you, you're so naïve."

"Quit acting like an asshole!" I screamed, throwing my fork down.

"No, I'm not an asshole. Angelo is for even looking at you. I fucking warned him."

Angelo nodded to Vito and Vinnie. They grabbed Matteo by the shoulders and held him back. I knew this day would come, but I didn't think it would be so soon. I should've known it was too good to be true.

"Tell me you haven't fucked her." Matteo whispered.

"I'm not a creep. And no, I haven't fucked her. I…"

"Tell me you haven't touched her."

Angelo sighed and closed his eyes. When he opened them back up, he narrowed his eyes. If looks could kill, my brother would be dead. "I haven't touched her."

That was a lie. The marks on my ass was proof of that.

"Tell me she doesn't sleep in your bed."

"Matteo, stop. You don't understand…"

"Oh, I understand completely. My sister is whoring around with my boss and best friend."

"Stop. It's not like that." I whispered, tears threatening to spill out.

"She's not a whore!" Angelo hissed, scooting his chair back. He stood up and leaned across the table. "Apologize."

"It's true. She's just like…"

"Quiet. Don't you dare finish that sentence." Vinnie growled.

"Fuck you, Matteo. I can't believe you!" I screamed.

I couldn't be here. Not when Matteo was being such an asshole. I stormed out of the room and ran upstairs. I entered my room, slamming my door. Tears streamed down my face. I wiped them away, but they kept on coming. The door opened, revealing Angelo. He wrapped his arms around my waist and kissed my temple. "He didn't mean any of that, Princess. He's just in shock."

"I hate him." I whispered.

"Don't say that." Angelo warned. "I don't ever want to hear you say that."

"But it's true. He's being a jerk."

Angelo twisted me around and cupped my face. "I know, but still, don't say you hate him. You never know what the future has in store for you. You could lose him and have to live with that for the rest of your life."

"Happy birthday to me. Yeah, me."

"It's your birthday?"

I nodded.

Angelo threw me a smirk. "So, you're eighteen now. Does Daddy need to give you a birthday spanking?"

I wrapped my arms around his neck and purred. "Maybe you do, Daddy."

"Don't tempt me, little girl. I still need to deal with your brother."

"Where is he?"

"He's gone to the club for the night. Said he would talk later."

"So, we're all alone?" I teased.

He lowered his hands and palmed my ass. Desire rippled through me as he brushed his lips against mine. I ran my hands through his hair as he deepened the kiss. Dominant Angelo was sexy as hell. And right now, I craved him more than ever. Especially after everything that happened.

"Fuck me, baby girl." Angelo groaned. "You taste so good."

"Take me, Angelo." I whispered.

He held my face and pressed his forehead against mine. "I can't. Matteo..."

"Fuck him. If he thinks I'm being a whore, then I'll be a whore."

"Watch your mouth, baby girl."

"I don't care."

Angelo pressed his lips into a thin line and narrowed his eyes. I knew I was being a brat, but I couldn't help it. I loved getting him all worked up. he ran his hands down my neck, stopping at my waist and squeezed. I gasped at the sudden contact.

"If it weren't for me not knowing Matteo was returning, I'd strip you and bend you over my knee, baby girl."

"Do it, Daddy. I. Dare. You."

He yanked me forward by the hips and whispered harshly in the ear. "Don't tempt me, little girl. You wouldn't like the punishment I have in store for you."

"You would spank me." I told him confidently.

Little did I know, that wasn't the case. Because he reached into his jacket and pulled out a silver butt plug. I swallowed hard as he pressed it against my lips. I felt a chill run down my back and my nipples hardened.

"Open your mouth, little girl."

I parted my lips and sucked the plug seductively. I never leave his eyes when I start to suck like it's his cock. He groaned as he retracted it and held my hips with one arm. "Bend over the bed and pull up your dress for Daddy. Punishment starts now."

"But…"

"Now." He growled. "I want you to bend over and pull up your dress. Spread those cheeks for Daddy."

I pleaded him with my eyes, but he led me to the bed and pushed me over the bed. I turned my head, throwing him one more glance.

"Eyes forward and spread your cheeks."

I took a deep breath and pulled up my dress. Now, I regret not wearing any panties. I spread my cheeks and felt him press the cold metal against my clit and groan. "So wet for me. Does Daddy excite you?"

"Mmm, yes Daddy."

He slid it into my heat and gathered my wetness on the plug. I arched my hips and moaned, throwing my head back. To my disappointment he pulled out and pressed it against my puckered hole. Angelo inched the plug inside me until it was all the way in. pain and pleasure caused me to cry out. He leaned over me and slapped his hand over my mouth and chuckled softly.

"Shh, baby girl. We don't want anyone to hear how desperate you are for Daddy, do we?"

I shook my head and moaned against his hand. He slid his free hand between my legs and pressed two fingers against my clit. He worked circles ferociously as he kissed my neck. His hardness pressed against my ass as he tortured me slowly with his mouth.

"You will wear this all day. Punishment for a filthy mouth and you will not touch yourself. That, baby girl, is your punishment. When I feel you've learned your lesson, I'll allow you to cum."

I whimpered and nodded my head.

Angelo pulled away and gave the butt plug a few taps. "Be a good girl for Daddy."

"Yes, Daddy."

I loved being his bad girl, but I craved those two words from him.

Good girl.

"Good girl. Go get cleaned up and whatever you do, do not remove the plug. Daddy says when to remove it."

Chapter 15

Angelo

I smiled when Vivianna slid into the car. She whimpered when her ass hit the leather seat. It pleased me to know she was a good girl. Vivianna changed into a short off the shoulder green dress. I leaned forward and instructed Vinnie, "Go to the hotel."

I can't wait to get her alone. I just hope that Matteo doesn't come home. I have so many things I want to try. I packed all kinds of toys to play with her with. She bit her lip and placed her hand on my thigh. She inched upward, causing me to internally groan. I gripped her wrist and growled. "Fucking tease!"

Vivianna brushed her lips against my neck and took my skin between her teeth. Vinnie glanced and me through the mirror and shook his head, chuckling. Yeah. He knew this was going to end in disaster. I didn't care though.

"Do you really think it's a good idea to tease Daddy, little girl?"

She ran her tongue up my neck and back down. Fuck. If only she knew what I had in store for her. The butt plug was just the beginning of her night. She would be stripped bare and tied up to the bed. By the end of the night, she would be begging Daddy to fuck her. And that's a decision I would have to make. Could I actually go through with it? Did I want to cross the line? I wanted to. I really did. But... Matteo made it clear that I wasn't to fuck her. My dick disagrees. If I did fuck her, it would only be between us two. And maybe Vinnie. He won't tell though.

"We're here." Vinnie says, stopping at the back entrance.

Vivianna is still sucking on my neck. I hate to pull her off me, but I need to get her to my suite. Preferably, without being noticed. Vivianna gasped when I grabbed the back of her neck and pulled away. "As much as I hate to do that, we're here. Come, baby girl. Daddy has a surprise for you."

I grabbed my overnight bag and slid out of the car, holding my hand out for her. She took it and batted her eyelashes. I yanked her to my chest and captured her lips. Just enough to leave her begging for more.

"Don't tease." She whined.

"You're not one to make demands, little girl. And don't think you're not getting punished for teasing me. Daddy doesn't like to be teased."

"Sorry, Daddy."

"Liar. That's two, baby girl. Do you want to keep going?"

She apologized again, but this time she had a devious grin. Yeah, she wasn't sorry. But she would be. Just as soon as I got her inside the room.

I took her inside, but to my surprise, we were met with a familiar face. Fuck me. No use lying to the man. I handed Vivianna the bag and the key card and whispered. "Go inside, I'll be right behind you."

Matteo cracked his neck and blew out a harsh breath. "You son of a bitch!"

He lunged for me, but I blocked his right hook. I countered with a punch to the jaw. God, he was angry. Not that I blame him. I was just about to take his sister to a hotel room. He told me he was going to the club. Apparently not. Or... he had a woman here himself. Or two. I knew Matteo liked to have threesomes. He didn't hide the fact either.

I stepped back and raised my hands in surrender. "Calm down."

"You were bringing her here, why? You were really going to fuck my sister here?!" he growled.

He lunged for me again. This time, I blocked him and lunged back. We tumbled to the floor. He wrapped his hands around my throat. As did I. He gasped for air when I tightened my hands around his neck. He did the same to me.

"Calm. The. Fuck. Down." I hissed through clenched teeth.

"End it."

He wasn't talking about ending his life. He was telling me to end what I had with Vivianna.

"Or what?"

"Or else... you can find yourself another second-in-command and best friend."

I loosened my grip and fell back on the floor. "Matteo..."

"You have two hours. End it or else you can find someone else to be your right-hand man."

"Matteo..." I whispered. "I... it's going to break her heart."

Mine too.
She would cry.
My heart would shatter.
And I would have to watch her settle down with someone else.

Matteo got up and dusted off his pants. "Two hours."

Either break my baby girl's heart or lose my best friend.
Not much of a choice.

Before Matteo entered the elevator, he turned to me and smirked. "I'll make sure she knows what a piece of shit you are. I'll let her know how much of a player you really are."

I swallowed hard as I stood up. Tonight was supposed to be a romantic night with my girl. I guess karma came to bite me in the ass. How was I going to let her down gently? Vivianna is sweet and loving, but if you piss her off, she's the fucking Devil Incarnate.
I knocked on the door and nearly gasped. From the looks of it, Vivianna heard everything. She was curled up on the bed, wiping her tears. She knew I had a choice to make. It was either her or him.

"Baby…"

"Go on, leave. I know what you're going to decide."

"I don't have a choice. Matteo…"

"I thought you were different. That we had something."

"We do, baby girl."

"Fuck you, Angelo Valentino. Just go, I'll find my own way home."

Walking away was harder than I thought.

Before I left I gave her one more lingering kiss and told her how sorry I was. I just hope she forgives me down the road. Not today. Not tomorrow. But sometime in the future, I would find a way to make her mine again. And next time, I won't walk away.

Soon, baby girl.
I'll find a way to make you my Queen.
But that day isn't today.

Sign up for my newsletter:

http://eepurl.com/dunalb

Copyright ©

2020 C. Davis-
All rights reserved

No part of this publication may be reproduced, distributed, or transmitted in an form or by any means, including photocopying, recording, or other electronic or mechanical methods, without the prior written permission of the publisher, except in the case of brief quotations embodied in critical reviews and certain other non-commercial uses permitted by the copyright law.

This is a work of fiction. All names, characters, places and specific instances are products of the author's imagination and used fictitiously. No actual reference to any real person, living or dead, is intended or inferred.

Made in the USA
Middletown, DE
18 April 2023

29005788R00046